I Like to Read® books, created by award-winning
picture book artists as well as talented newcomers,
instill confidence and the joy of reading in new readers.

We want to hear every new reader say, "I like to read!"

Visit our website for flash cards and activities:
www.holidayhouse.com/ILiketoRead
#ILTR
This book has been tested by an educational expert
and determined to be a guided reading level G.

HORSE & BUGGY

PAINT IT OUT!

Ethan Long

I Like to Read®

HOLIDAY HOUSE • NEW YORK

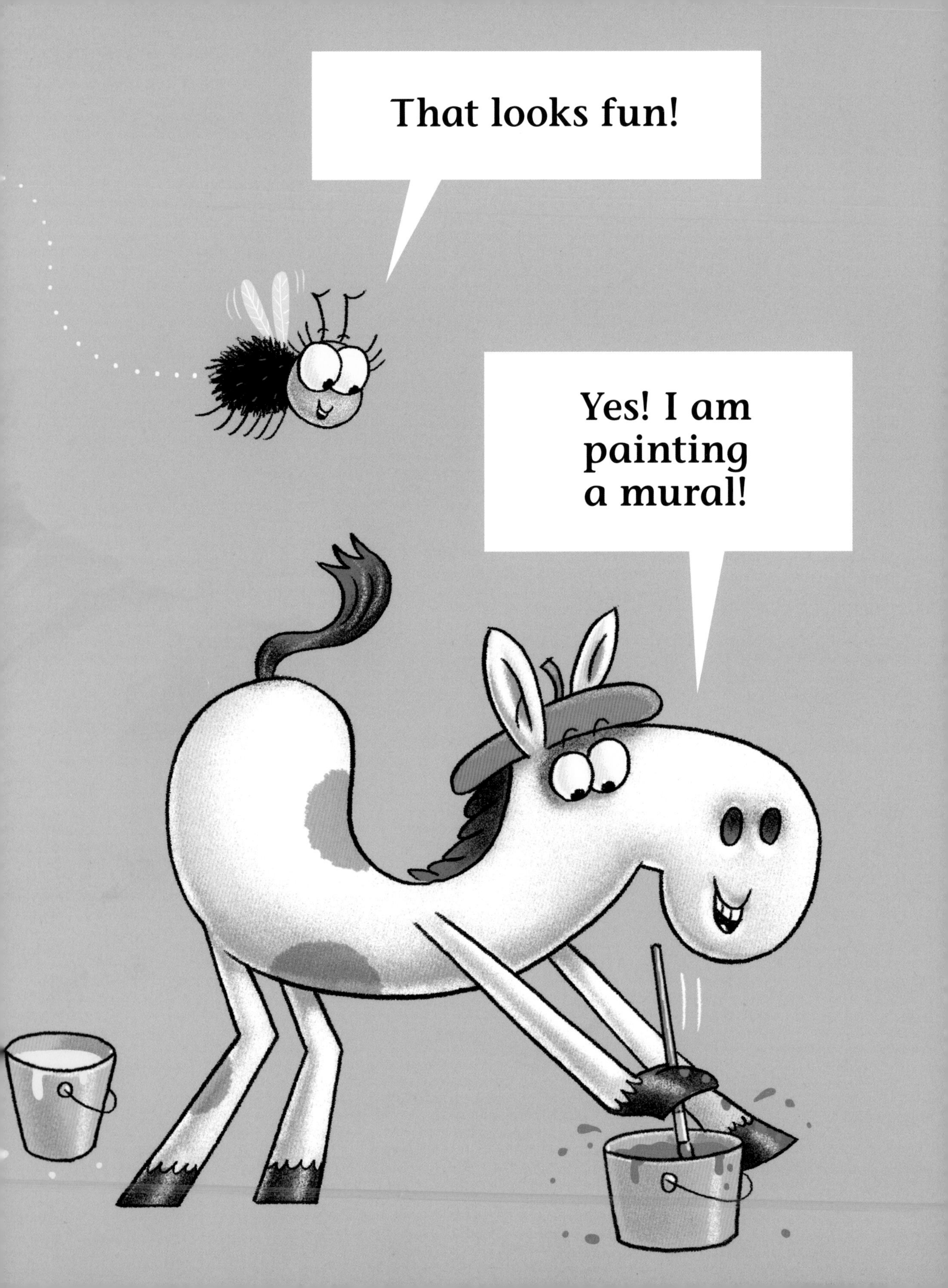
That looks fun!
Yes! I am painting a mural!

Plunk!

1. Get a drop cloth.

2. Put your things on it.

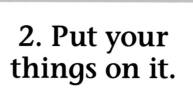